In
Egyptian Times

Edited by Anna Milbourne
With thanks to Dr. Anne Millard for information about Ancient Egypt

This edition first published in 2014 by Usborne Publishing Ltd, 83-85 Saffron Hill, London EC1N 8RT, England.
www.usborne.com Copyright © 2014, 2009 Usborne Publishing Ltd.

In
Egyptian
Times

Kate Davies

Illustrated by Alfredo Belli

Designed by Laura Wood

Have you ever heard of Egypt?

Long ago in this hot, dusty land,
everyone lived by the cool River Nile.

Early each morning,
a family would go outside
to praise the rising sun.

Then they sat in the shade
to eat their breakfast.

After breakfast, a little girl
had lessons at home...

while her brother
hurried off...

past men catching fish in the River Nile...

and farmers working in their fields...

...all the way to school.

"You're late,"
his teacher scolded.

He sat down with the other boys
and the writing lesson began.

The boys dipped their brushes in ink
and carefully copied out the words.

The word for
water looked
like waves.

Hand was an
outstretched palm.

Mouth looked
like a pair of lips.

After school, the children wandered through the bustling market.

Acrobats leaped and tumbled.

The smell of spices filled the air.

But best of all were the sticky-sweet honey cakes.

Nearby, people were flocking to the riverbank...

to see the Pharaoh's boat arrive.

The children peered through the crowd
to catch a glimpse of their king.

The Pharaoh was carried through the streets
on a gleaming golden throne.

Servants kept him cool
with ostrich-feather fans...

and women scattered
sweet-smelling petals in his path.

That night the family had a party
to celebrate the Pharaoh coming home.

Everyone feasted on
roast goose and juicy ribs...

and crispy fish in palm leaves.

Then the little boy
played a boardgame
with his friends...

while his sister
strummed her harp
and sang.

As the sky grew inky-dark
and the buzz of crickets filled the air...

the family said goodbye
to all their guests.

The yawning children went upstairs
and rolled their mats out on the roof.

They went to sleep beneath the starry sky...

...and dreamed of all they'd seen that day.

Would you like to have lived
in Egyptian Times?